Antero de Quental, Edgar Prestage

Anthero de Quental

sixty-four sonnets Englished by Edgar Prestage

.

Antero de Quental, Edgar Prestage

Anthero de Quental

sixty-four sonnets Englished by Edgar Prestage

ISBN/EAN: 9783337190767

Printed in Europe, USA, Canada, Australia, Japan

Cover: Foto ©Andreas Hilbeck / pixelio.de

More available books at **www.hansebooks.com**

ANTHERO DE QUENTAL

ANTHERO DE QUENTAL

SIXTY-FOUR SONNETS

ENGLISHED BY

ÉDGAR PRESTAGE

BALLIOL COLLEGE, OXFORD

CORR. MEMBER OF THE LISBON

GEOGRAPHICAL SOCIETY: EDITOR

OF 'THE LETTERS OF A

PORTUGUESE NUN'

ETC. ETC.

LONDON

PUBLISHED BY DAVID NUTT

IN THE STRAND

1894

Edinburgh: T. and A. CONSTABLE
Printers to Her Majesty

TO MY FRIENDS

THEOPHILO BRAGA

LUCIANO CORDEIRO, JOAQUIM DE ARAUJO

XAVIER DA CUNHA, JAYME BATALHA REIS

TOMMASO CANNIZZARO, GÖRAN BJORKMAN

MAXIME FORMONT

PREFACE

NCOURAGED *by the ready welcome given to my version of the 'Lettres de la Religieuse Portugaise,'*[1] *which was an attempt to bring one of the masterpieces of Portuguese literature to the notice of Englishmen, I now introduce a very different character*

[1] *The Letters of a Portuguese Nun (Marianna Alcoforado).* Translated by Edgar Prestage. London, 1893.

vii

from the love-lorn Nun of Beja. Anthero de Quental, the Philosopher-Mystic, is one of the three distinguished poets that Portugal has produced in this century—the others being Almeida Garrett and João de Deus—and his Sonnets are, excepting those of Camoens, the finest in the language. As regards their subject, they illustrate some important phases of modern European thought as well as show the various philosophical stages through which their author passed, while in form they are perfect of their kind, Anthero having, like Petrarch, spent years over the labor limae. *Critics, to*

quote the words of Anthero himself, will be interested to observe
in them the effects of Germanism
on the unprepared mind of a South
European, and the poems, as he
suggests, cannot fail to attract the
attention of all who study the comparative psychology of nations.

Their exceptional merit has
indeed been already widely recognised, and translations of the
whole or a part of them exist in
French, Swedish, Italian, German,
and Spanish, while a Polish version is understood to be in prepara-
tion. Such being the case, it is
unfortunate that they should not
yet have found an English trans-

lator, or at least one better able than myself to do them justice, for, it has been truly said,

'Let Poets be by Poets read,
By Poets be interpreted
Their works divine !'

Out of the one hundred and nine Sonnets collected and published by my friend Senhor Oliveira Martins[1] *I have selected sixty-four for translation here. My aim has been to give such as are most characteristic of their author, or most striking in themselves; and I have consequently rejected those that seemed to be of less*

---

[1] *Os Sonetos Completos de Anthero de Quental.* Publicados por J. P. Oliveira Martins. Porto, 1886. 2nd ed. 1890.

*interest or merit. But nearly all
are worthy of an English dress, at
least from one point of view,
namely, that they form a com-
mentary on the intellectual life of
the poet, and enable us to understand better one of the most re-
markable men of the time, called,
not inaptly, the Portuguese Heine.*

*In the present version I have
kept as closely as possible to the
original, and in most cases the
translation is line for line. I
preferred, if necessary, to sacrifice
form rather than matter, and to
appear bald rather than give a
paraphrase, my reason being that
these Sonnets are not the work*

of a mere Parnassian, but of a
Philosopher who laid bare his
thoughts, and a Mystic who re-
corded his dreams in this par-
ticular form. Nearly all of them
are here published for the first
time, the only exceptions being
six reprinted from the 'Academy,'
and a few others that have already
appeared in Portuguese papers.

The portrait facing the title-
page is reproduced from a photo-
graph taken shortly before Anthero's death, and I am indebted
to Senhor Oliveira Martins for the
loan of the original.

The Introduction, which is only
designed to supplement the Auto-

biography, will, I hope, be found to contain sufficient about the life and work of the poet for a due comprehension of his Sonnets. Following this comes the Auto-biography in the form of a letter addressed by Anthero to Dr. Storck, his German translator, and since it is a particularly valuable document, both for the literary critic and the psychologist, I need not apologise for its insertion.

Lastly, I have to thank my friends Mr. York Powell, Mr. Hutchings of Ealing, and Mr. Oliver Elton of Owens College, Manchester, for many a suggestion and emendation; but for their

ANTHERO DE QUENTAL

kindly help the present version would have been far more lame and faulty than it actually is.

EDGAR PRESTAGE.

CHILTERN, BOWDON, 1894.

CONTENTS

INTRODUCTION

A

Only a breath divides faith and unfaith,
  only a breath divides belief from doubt.
                          OMAR KHAYYAM.

INTRODUCTION

Ave da morte, que piando agouros
Tinges meus ares de funereo luto!
Ave da morte (que em teus ais a escuto)
Meus dias murcharás, mas não meus louros:
Doou—me Phebo aos seculos vindouros,
Deponho a flor da vida, e guardo o fructo,
Pagando em vil materia um vão tributo,
Retenho a posse de immortaes thesouros.

BOCAGE, Sonnet cccxlviii.

NTHERO DE QUENTAL
was born in the year 1842
at St. Michael in the
Azores, an island that has
given distinguished writers
to modern Portugal, in-
cluding Theophilo Braga[1] and our Poet.

---

[1] This Introduction is founded on Dr. Theophilo Braga's exhaustive work *As Modernas Ideias na Litteratura Portugueza*, Lisboa, 1893, as well as on Senhor Oliveira Martins' Preface to the *Sonetos Completos*.

His family was a good one, and his father a man of position and talent. His mother, a fervent Catholic, brought him up strictly, but the influence of heredity joined to a hostile environment proved too strong, and Anthero soon left the beaten track. The revolutionary and mystical tendencies which he exhibited in after life were inherited, the former from his grandfather, a friend of the poet Bocage, and the latter from his ancestor, Padre Bartholomeu de Quental, a well-known seventeenth-century writer and preacher, and the founder of the Portuguese Oratorians.

After spending a short time at school in Lisbon under the poet Antonio Feliciano de Castilho, whose authority in the world of letters he was in after years so effectually to destroy, Anthero was sent to the University of Coimbra in 1854, and there he led a Bohemian existence, and never studied systematically.

His early poems show him to have been the disciple of Lamartine, Herculano, and Soares de Passos, but this was merely a transient phase. Before long he had the misfortune to lose his faith in Christianity under the influence of the revolutionary metaphysicians whose works he then read, and he became the head of those students who were bent on the same study, and leader of all the more disorderly elements in the University. An incident which happened at this time, and did more than anything else to confirm his *prestige*, is perhaps not unworthy of mention. Prince Humbert, now King of Italy, happened to visit Coimbra while on his European tour, and Anthero was chosen by the general body of students to welcome him in their name. In the presence of the chief authorities of the place who had assembled to greet the Prince, he bluntly and boldly said, 'We have not come here to welcome you as the son of King Victor Emanuel and heir to the throne of Italy, but as the friend of Garibaldi.'

In spite, however, of his turbulence and eccentricity, it was not long before Anthero exhibited signs of great and unusual poetical talent. Allusion has already been made to his early verse of a religious character, all of which he afterwards destroyed, and it is now time to mention the Sonnets of the first period [1] (1860-1862), which contain in embryo all his later sentiments and ideas, while belonging to no one school. Anthero, it should be mentioned, adopted the form of

---

[1] The Sonnets published by Senhor Oliveira Martins in the *Sonetos Completos* were divided by him into five periods. This arrangement has been preserved in the present version, and is referred to above and elsewhere.

the Sonnet under the influence of João de
Deus, whom he now proclaimed the foremost
Portuguese poet for three centuries, and the
inheritor of the tradition left by the great
Camoens.

These first Sonnets of his are deistic in
religion, but that to the 'Unknown God'
shows how fantastic and shadowy his ideas
on the subject then were. They contain a
medley of hope and despair, although the
latter predominates, yet they are impregnated
at times with a tender melancholy, and
marked by none of the violent affirmations
and denials that characterise the productions
of later years. The poet is on the search for
a God, but a being of a strange order; he
seeks certainty and sees the vanity of all
things; he fluctuates to and fro and is
'blown about by every wind of doctrine.' For
a moment Platonic Love presents itself as

a possible solution, but he finally decides that

'The greatest ill is ever to have lived.'

The struggle against Destiny has proved to be vain, Christianity seems to him a failure, and he cries out in his despair,

'Perhaps there may be happiness *sans* hope.'

From the tone of his earlier Sonnets it is plain that pessimism had taken a firm hold of Anthero, and indeed it never afterwards left him.

It was while a student at Coimbra that he first distinguished himself as a pamphleteer, a branch in which he outstripped all rivals, and one for which his *ingenium* particularly fitted him. His literary style, it may be remarked in passing, is excellent, and his prose the best since the days of Almeida Garrett, that of the *Considerações*

INTRODUCTION

sobre a Philosophia da Historia Litteraria Portugueza being especially worthy of praise.

In 1864 he completed his law course at the University, but stayed on for another year, a victim to nostalgia, and without a plan for the future. He was chiefly occupied in making a selection of his best poems, and these he published in 1865 under the title of *Odes Modernas*. The book, which includes many of his Sonnets, is inspired by the revolutionary and freethinking ideal, and reveals the influence of Victor Hugo in the *Châtiments*. Many of the pieces it contains are, like 'Á Historia,' powerful in conception as well as beautiful in expression, while others are both far-fetched and weak.

The second series of Sonnets (1862-1866), written about this time, forms a marked contrast to the *Odes Modernas*. While psychologically the least original, it is, as

Oliveira Martins remarks, artistically the
most brilliant, and includes such compositions as the 'Eastern Dream,' the 'Idyll,'
'Velut Umbra,' and the 'Palace of Happiness.' With much that is peaceful and
natural there are yet some jarring notes.
The poet hungers still, and is not satisfied,
for, to adopt his own words, 'the fever of
the Ideal is wasting him.' But an under-
current of resignation pervades his occasional
throes of despair, and he perceives that he
should have braced himself up for the
struggle of life, and not lived, as he has, in
'dreams and anxiousness.' To this phase
there succeeds one of satire, and the series
ends with the noble sonnet entitled 'A
Romantic Burying-Place,' in which, by means
of a symbol, the poet prays for annihilation
and absorption into the Universal Whole.
This has been called his Baudelaire and

Espronceda period, and here they stopped,
but it proved to be only a stage in Anthero's
philosophical pilgrimage.

In 1865 began the famous Coimbra
Question, from which sprang the school of
that name, as well as the wonderful revival
of Portuguese literature our day has seen.
At first it consisted of a reaction on the
part of the rising generation against the
poet Castilho, who, ever since the death of
Garrett and the retirement of Herculano,
had reigned supreme in the world of letters
and denied an entrance to those who re-
fused to do him homage ; but it ended by
proclaiming the death of Ultra-Romanti-
cism, and by opening a new era to Portuguese thought.[1] Castilho was a man of

[1] The specific offence of which Castilho had been guilty,
and the one that did more than anything else to discredit him
with Young Portugal, was his severe and unjust criticism of the
Lusiads in his Preface to the *D. Jayme* of Thomaz Ribeiro.

another age, an 'old Arcadian' as Anthero called him, who knew nothing of modern ideas, and whose sole claim to distinction rested on the fact of his being a first-class artist in language. Theophilo Braga with the *Visão dos Tempos*, inspired by Victor Hugo's *Legende des Siècles*, struck the first blow at Castilho and his Mutual Praise School, and Anthero followed. Then a regular pamphlet war broke out, and for a time the Coimbra Question formed the chief and almost the only topic of conversation. It must be confessed that João de Deus was the true precursor of the new school that arose out of the defeat of Castilho, but Theophilo Braga and Anthero de Quental were its actual founders, though the latter retired from the contest before it was half over, having neither the perseverance nor the energy necessary to carry through a great movement.

INTRODUCTION

In 1867 and the following years Anthero travelled in France and the United States, and during his stay in the former country visited both Michelet and Renan. On returning to Lisbon he took up the Iberian Question, which was then agitating men's minds, and wrote a pamphlet on the subject, but soon gave it up in favour of Socialism. He became convinced that literature could never of itself regenerate Portugal, and therefore, in conjunction with a Swiss named Fontana, he organised the Portuguese Socialists, and began a series of Conferences at the Lisbon Casino, which, however, the Government quickly suppressed on the ground that they were dangerous. But they could never have resulted in good, for, at this time, Anthero's philosophy was entirely destructive, and he spoke of revolutions as 'the Christianity of the modern world.' His

'Programme of Work for the New Generation,' that had been so much talked about,
never appeared, and deserting both Socialism
and Society he retired within himself.

In the Sonnets of this latter period (1864-
1874) the mind of the philosopher reacts on
the temperament of the poet, and a system
is gradually evolved out of the old fury. For
though he is now, as Oliveira Martins ob-
serves, both a Nihilist in philosophy and an
Anarchist in politics, it is evidently but a
passing phase. He tends more and more to
emancipate himself from the nebulosity of
the first two periods, and finally decides
that the 'Summum Bonum' is to be found
only in the Conscience. He now begins to
see clearly where others only grope, and his
poems become sculptural and Dantesque.[1]

---

[1] Anthero was a student of Dante, and translated part of
Canto VI. of the *Purgatorio* into Portuguese.

INTRODUCTION

His pessimism is systematic, and his atheism resolves itself into a keen but kindly sarcasm. The period which embraces the next six years (1874-1880) is one of transcendental irony. 'What is man?' he asks, and answers, 'A luckless mixture of light and darkness,' or 'perhaps no one,' and the same note is struck in several compositions of this series. The 'Convert' shows traces of remorse for the past, but ends

'I only need to know if God exists.'

Now too he begins to idealise Death, as in the fine sonnets, 'Mors Liberatrix' and 'Mors-Amor,' and announces himself a Stoic. He proclaims metempsychosis in 'the Circus,' and the result of his study of Buddhism appears in the sonnet entitled ' Nirvâna,' and he winds up by declaring in a tone of sad conviction that it is not worth while having lived.

The fifth and last period extends from

1880 to 1884. Anthero was now near the end, and had learnt that there is no satisfaction for the soul on earth, and, in the series of sonnets entitled 'In Praise of Death,' his one desire is to escape from existence. He welcomes Death in a spirit of faith, nay, of eager expectancy—for is not *non-being* the only true *being*? He has now left forms behind, and sees their essences, the world is smoke before him, and in 'Lacrymae Rerum' and 'Redemption' he hears all things in Nature sighing for the hour of their deliverance. Everything is vain, except Love, which survives all else ; and Nirvâna, which is liberty, is his ideal, with Love as its mediator. Finally, Death invites the toilers to repose, and in the last sonnet of the collection Anthero rests 'in the hand of God.'

On his retirement from the world of action the poet had gone to Oporto, and there made the acquaintance of Senhor Oliveira Martins, who became his *alter ego*. It is to this friend-ship that the collection and publication of the Sonnets, as well as the perspicuous Pre-face which .accompanies them, are owing. Anthero, however, tired of Oporto before long, and, being desirous of more privacy than a city afforded, he transferred himself to Villa do Conde, sixteen miles off, where he lived in complete solitude and in a state of moral depression in which all action was distasteful to him. His life's work was now over, and his last public appearance took place on the formation of the ' Liga Patriotica do Norte,' [1] when he was dragged from retirement to

---

[1] This League was founded after the British Ultimatum of January 1890, which proved to be the first step in the spoliation of Portugal's Central African provinces, and showed how little, despite Mr. Herbert Spencer, the great principle of Justice was understood by our statesmen. Had Garrett been alive at the time he would assuredly have erased from his *Camões* the lines in which he names England ' senhora de justiça.'

lend the sanction of his presence to the attempt to unite the North of Portugal in a society for resisting English aggression, but he soon found himself out of his element and withdrew. In 1891 he passed through Lisbon on his way to the Azores, and, as though he had a presentiment of death, deposited his family treasure, the MS. of the works of Padre Bartholomeu de Quental, with Senhor Oliveira Martins for presentation to the Academy of Sciences. On reaching St. Michael his spinal disease, which had been pronounced incurable, became worse, and, lacking, as he did, faith in God, he fell a victim to final despair and shot himself in the public square of Ponta Delgada, on September 11th, 1891.

From what has gone before it will be seen that the poems of Anthero de Quental are

mainly psychological, and give evidence of
the perpetual strife at work within him.
Like poor Marianna, the Nun of Beja, he
is 'torn asunder by a thousand contrary
emotions,' and is ever striving after the Ideal.
Though wonderfully versatile as a writer, the
conflict between his imaginative and reasoning
powers which was always going on, without either being strong enough to overcome
the other, proved a source of weakness and
robbed him of energy. His misfortunes, too,
were in great measure fancied rather than
actual, although it is true that his later years
were rendered miserable by neurosis. His
agony was chiefly that of the mind, caused
by regarding the perpetual misery of the
world that reflected itself within him, and he
exemplifies the pregnant line of Victor Hugo :

' Un poëte est un monde enfermé dans un homme.'

His religious ideal, if so it may be called,

consisted of a Hellenism crowned by a Buddhism, and of this the Autobiography speaks more at length. Few men of his generation have exercised a greater and more subtle influence for weal or woe on the minds of his countrymen than Anthero de Quental, and no man was more beloved and revered by those that knew him. Among his friends, indeed, he was called ' Saint Anthero,' a title which his asceticism and charity did something to explain, and scarcely a man of note visited Oporto without making a pilgrimage to the poet's humble cottage at Villa do Conde.

The time has not yet arrived, nor is this the place, for a critical estimate of the value of his work, but it may safely be said that he will rank with the foremost poets of the nineteenth century, in the company of Heine and Leopardi.

INTRODUCTION

Such then was the man, a selection from whose masterpiece is here presented for the kindly consideration of the English public, a poet whose device might well have been those lines of the sweet singer Christovam Falcão :

> 'All discretion doth consist
> In man knowing soon as may be
> That no pleasure maketh happy,
> For the course of life is triste.'[1]

---

[1] 'Toda a descriçam consiste
em saber homem com cedo
que nenhum prazer faz ledo
pois o seer da vida he triste.'
                            Cantigas.

AUTOBIOGRAPHY

' Tutti gli uomini d'ogni sorte, che hanno fatto qualche
cosa che sia virtuosa, o si veramente che le virtu
somigli, doverieno, essendo veritieri e da bene, di
      lor propia mano descrivere la loro vita.'—
          Vita di Benvenuto Cellini, lib. 1.

AUTOBIOGRAPHY

PONTA DELGADA,
ISLAND OF ST. MICHAEL, AZORES,
14*th May* 1887.

EAR SIR,[1]—The biographical and bibliographical information that you ask for may be compressed into the following narrative. I was born in this Island of St. Michael in April 1842, and am a descendant of one of the oldest families of colonists here. I have therefore completed my forty-

---

[1] This autobiographical letter was written by Anthero to Dr. Storck, the German translator of the Sonnets, as mentioned in the Preface. Dr. Theophilo Braga printed it from the MS. in his *Raios de extincta luz*, Lisboa, 1892, and it is here translated verbatim, save for a few lines at the beginning and end, that consist of personal references and only concern the addressee.

fifth year. I studied at the University of
Coimbra from 1856 to 1864, and took my
degree of *baccalaureus juris* there, but I confess that it was not the study of law that
interested me or absorbed my attention during those years, for I was and have remained
an indifferent lawyer.

What had an important, and probably the
most decisive influence on my life at that
time, was the kind of intellectual and moral
revolution that I underwent, when, but a
shy youth, I found myself all at once torn
away from the almost patriarchal existence
of a distant province, whose history was a
record of undisturbed repose, and thrown
into the midst of the merciless intellectual
excitement of a centre where the conflict-
ing currents of modern thought came, more
or less, into collision. In a moment my
Catholic education, with all its traditions, was

swept away, and I fell into a condition of doubt and uncertainty that affected me the more from my being naturally of a religious turn of mind, and born to believe calmly, and obey without questioning, an established authority. I found myself without a guide ; a dreadful state of mind, and one in which nearly all my contemporaries more or less shared, when, for the first time in Portugal, the path of tradition was deliberately and consciously abandoned.

If you add to this an ardent imagination, with which I had been exuberantly endowed by Nature, the awakening of the amorous passions that marks early manhood, the impetuosity and presumption, the excitability and despondency of a Southern temperament, much straightforwardness and honesty of purpose, but a great lack of perseverance and method, you will have an idea of my capabilities and shortcomings on my entering, at the age of eighteen, into the great world of thought and poetry.

Amid the desultory reading to which I then abandoned myself, devouring with an equal zest novels and books of natural science, poets, publicists, and even theologians, the perusal of Goethe's *Faust*, in the French translation of Blaze de Bury, and Rémusat's book on the recent German Philosophy, made a deep and lasting impression on my mind. I was definitely won over to the German school of thought, and if, among French writers, I gave the preference to Proudhon and Michelet, it was doubtless because these two breathed most of all the spirit of beyond the Rhine. I subsequently read much of Hegel in Vera's French translation, for it was not until a later time that I learnt German. I do not know whether I rightly understood him ; my independence of mind, too, revolted against acknowledging a master, but I was certainly carried away by the imposing tendencies of his great synthesis. At any rate, Hegelianism was the starting-point of my philosophical speculations, and I may justly say that my intellectual development took place in accordance with its tenets.

How, though, did I reconcile this devotion to the doctrines of the apologist of the Prussian State with the Radicalism and Socialism of Michelet, Quinet, and Proudhon? These are mysteries of youthful incoherence of thought ! Certain, however, it is, that, arrayed in this armour, more brilliant than enduring, I confidently entered the arena. I wanted to reform everything—I, who had not even half completed my own education. I employed a good deal of industry and some talent that might have been devoted to a better purpose, in newspaper articles, pamphlets, manifestoes, and revolutionary conferences. At the same time that I was conspiring to bring about the Iberian Union, I was founding, on the other hand, Trades Unions, and, being a disciple of Marx and Engels, introduced the International Association of Workmen into Portugal. Hence for about seven or eight years I was a sort of Lasalle on a small scale, and had my hour of vain popularity.

All that I can remember of what I then published is as follows. My first pamphlet dates from the year 1864. It is called *A Defence of the Encyclical of His Holiness Pope Pius IX. against so-called Liberal Opinions.*[1] It is a protest against the illogi-

---

[1] *Defensa da Carta Encyclica de S.S. Pio IX. contra a chamada opinião liberal.*

cal position taken up by the Liberal Press, which attacked the Syllabus, and yet professed at the same time to be strictly Catholic. The author, while extolling the Pope for what was admirable in his uncompromising attitude towards the spirit of the age, recognised in this very attitude an historical law, and reverently intoned a 'De Profundis' for the Church, doomed (*sic!*) by the very sublimity of its institution, to fall unscathed, but not to give way, and he attacked the insincerity of the Liberal papers.

My last pamphlet is dated 1871. It is entitled *A Letter to His Excellency the Marquis of Avila and Bolama, concerning his Edict putting an end to the Conferences at the Lisbon Casino*.[1] These democratic

---

[1] *Carta ao Exmo Marquez de Avila e Bolama, sobre a Portaria que mandou fechar as Conferencias do Casino lisbonense.*

31

Conferences had been set on foot by me with the co-operation of a group of young men, almost all of whom are now well known in politics, and they were well attended by the better class of working men. The Government, however, considered them dangerous, and arbitrarily put a stop to them. My pamphlet appears to have contributed, as was then rumoured, to the fall of the ministry, though indeed it could not have lasted long, since it was one of those that are called Transition Ministries. The pamphlet is a diatribe, but an eloquent one.

Between these two dates occurred the famous Literary or Coimbra Question, which for more than six months kept our small literary world in agitation, and was the source from which the present development of Portuguese literature took its rise. In-

and philology, who, owing to their presumption and want of respect, inspired perhaps little confidence, but who were unquestionably possessed of talent and honesty, and from whom, moreover, something might be expected when they should have settled down.

Facts have confirmed this impression. For of the ten or twelve names that stand highest in the literature of to-day, all, with the exception of two or three, belonged to the Coimbra School, or have been influenced by it. Germanism had obtained a firm footing in Portugal, and a new era began for Portuguese thought. The old Portugal, which had so far been kept artificially alive by a conventional literature, was dead at last. I was the standard-bearer of this kind of revolution, and, though I am not conceited about it, I cannot say either that I regret it. If an artificial order of things was

succeeded by a sort of anarchy, the latter
was, even so, preferable, containing as it did
germs of life, while nothing at all could be
expected from the former. To this period
further belongs the pamphlet entitled *The
Dignity of Letters and Official Literature.*[1]
I spent the year 1867 and part of 1868
travelling in France and Spain, and I visited
the United States of America. At the end
of the latter year I published the pamphlet
Portugal in face of the Spanish Revolution.[2]
In it I advocated the Iberian Union by
means of a Federal Republic, which was
then represented in Spain by Castelar, Pi y
Margall, and the majority of the Constituent
Assembly. It was a great delusion, which
I only abandoned, like many others of that

[1] *A Dignidade das Lettras e as Litteraturas officiaes.*
Lisboa, 1865.
[2] *Portugal perante a Revolução de Hespanha.*

period, after experience with its rude and oft-repeated lessons had compelled me to do so. So hard is it to correct a sort of false idealism in social matters.

My *Treatise on the Causes of the Decadence of the Peninsular Peoples in the Seventeenth and Eighteenth Centuries*,[1] although based on firmer premises, and on historical facts, still showed many traces of the influence of preconceived political ideas and biassed historical criticism. It dates from the year 1871. In that and the following year I took an active part in the Socialist movement which began in Lisbon, and wrote a good deal for political papers both in that city and in Oporto. At the same time I published a series of studies in a little volume under the title of *Re-*

---

[1] *Discurso sobre as causas da decadencia dos Povos peninsulares nos seculos XVII. e XVIII.*

*flections on the Philosophy of Portuguese Lit-
erary History.*[1] I believe that this is still
the best, or at least the most rational, of my
prose works. But I honestly confess to you
that I attach very small importance to all
these occasional writings of mine, and that,
at times, even, I can hardly refrain from
feeling ashamed of myself, for having published so much without having given more
thought to it. And for all that I met with
applause! Why? First of all, as I believe, because those who applauded me
were, in reality, neither deeper nor juster
thinkers than myself. Then again because
nature had given me a talent for Portuguese
prose, not for the conventional sort that
apes the style of the seventeenth and

[1] *Considerações sobre a Philosophia da Historia Litteraria
Portugueza (a proposito d'alguns livros recentes)*, por Anthero
de Quental. Porto-Braga, 1872.

eighteenth centuries, but for one having its model in the language actually in use at the present day, analytical certainly in the mode of development, but always and altogether Portuguese in expression. It pleased, for it was suited to the time, and, to speak briefly, I ended by being cited as a model prose-writer. The fact, however, remains, that these are all occasional writings, and that, so far, I have not produced anything in prose that can be called a work,—that is to say, something original, individual, and the result of study. I have long known how to write, but it was not until I attained forty-five that I found something to write about. Therefore let us leave behind us all this medley, which I only mention in compliance with your request for bibliographical information, and let us pass on to Poetry.

Besides the collection of Sonnets with which you are acquainted, I have published two other books. One of them, which appeared in 1872 under the title *Romantic Springtimes*,[1] contains my juvenilia, love-poems, and fancy pieces, written almost entirely between 1860 and 1865, that lay dispersed through various periodicals, and were not collected by me until 1872, when they appeared in book form together with several later productions similar in style. Perhaps I can best characterise this volume if I describe it in French as 'du Heine de deuxième qualité.' As many persons in this country have been struck by the similarity, it is not unworthy of remark. The second part of the *Complete Sonnets*, which contains pieces of this period only, will give you an adequate idea of its tenor

---

[1] *Primaveras Romanticas.* Versos dos vinte annos (1861-1864) por Anthero de Quental. Porto, 1872.

and style, just as the third part will of the *Modern Odes*,[1] the first edition of which appeared in 1865. I do not know precisely how to characterise this book. It is certainly above mediocrity, for it contains real passion and elevation of thought, but, besides being declamatory and abstract, it is indistinct at times, and fails to express clearly and typically the condition of mind to which the poems owe their existence. What however it does show clearly enough is the peculiar combination, already alluded to, of Hegel's naturalism, and Radical French humanitarianism. It is above all what the French term 'poésie de combat': behind the poet glimpses are caught of the pamphleteer, and the Church, the Monarchy, and the great men of the world are apostrophised by him in the character of an ideal leveller. In other

[1] *Odes Modernas*, 1st edition 1865, 2nd edition 1875.

poems, certainly, a calmer tone prevails, and in these the philosophical intent of the book appears, indefinite, it is true, but humane and elevated. The novelty, the boldness, may be even the undecided tone of thought, only vaguely idealist and humanitarian, made the fortune of the book with the rising generation, which proves, at least, that it was well timed, and that is about all I can say of it. To this cycle belong the Sonnets contained in the third part of the *Complete Sonnets*, many of which had already appeared in the *Modern Odes*. In the year 1874[1] the latter book went through a second edition, vastly improved, and enlarged by several new pieces. I consider this edition, such as it now is, and in spite of the defects inseparable from work of this kind, definitive.

---

[1] Its imprint is of the next year, 1875.

AUTOBIOGRAPHY

In that same year of 1874 I fell danger-
ously ill of a nervous complaint from which
I never thoroughly recovered. The conse-
quent enforced idleness, the prospect of
approaching death, the ruin of many ambitious plans, and a certain sensitiveness
peculiar to those that suffer from neurosis,
again, and more imperatively than ever
before, brought me face to face with the great
problem of existence. My past life seemed
to have been unprofitable, and existence on
the whole incomprehensible. The poems
that make up the fourth part (1874-1880) of
my little book, as well as many others that I
afterwards destroyed—those only remaining
which Oliveira Martins published in his introduction to the Sonnets,—bear witness to the
struggle that I was then engaged in for five
or six years with my own thoughts and feelings, both driving me to a barren pessimism

and despair. You know them, and therefore I need not explain them to you. I will only remark, however, that this evolution of feeling corresponded with an evolution of thought. Naturalism, however sublime and harmonious, even that of Goethe or Hegel, affords no real solution, for it leaves the conscience in suspense, and the mind unsatisfied, as regards everything in which it is most deeply interested. Its religiousness is false and lies merely on the surface ; at bottom it is nothing more than an intellectual and refined form of Paganism. Thus I strove in despair, without being able to overstep the bounds of Naturalism, within which my intellect had been born and developed. It made up the very air I breathed, and yet I felt as if it stifled me. Naturalism in its empirical and scientific form is 'the struggle for life,' a horrible strife, in which every man's hand is against his neighbour amid universal blindness ; in its transcendental form it is a cold and barren course of dialectics or a selfishly contemplative Epicureanism. Such were the consequences I then saw result from the doctrine on which I had been brought up, from my *alma mater*, so to speak, when I questioned it with the gravity and earnestness of one who before dying at least wishes to know what he came into the world for.

The reaction of my moral forces, and a fresh quickening of thought, preserved me from despair. At the same time, perceiving that the voice of moral consciousness cannot be the only unmeaning one amid the innumerable voices of the universe, I found, on reforming my philosophical education, that point of view confirmed, whether I referred to doctrines or to history. I now

diligently resumed the perusal of works on
philosophy, such as those of Hartmann,
Lange, and Du Bois-Reymond, and, hark-
ing back to the sources of German thought,
Leibnitz and Kant. More than this, I read
the ancient and modern moralists and mystical writers, especially the Theologia Ger-
manica, and Buddhist literature. I found
that mysticism, as the last word of psychological development, must naturally correspond
with the deepest essence of things, unless
the human conscience be an incongruity in
the system of the universe.

Naturalism struck me not as the final
explanation of things, but merely as the
outer system, the law of phenomena, the
phenomenology of Being. In Psychism,
that is, in good and in moral freedom, I
found the final and true explanation, not
only of moral man, but of all nature, even

in its physical and elementary moments. Leibnitz's Monadology, properly emended, lends itself perfectly to this idea of the world, at once naturalistic and spiritual. The spirit is the type of reality ; nature is no more than a distant imitation, a vague mimicry, a dim and imperfect symbol of the spirit. Goodness, therefore, is the supreme law of the universe, and the essence of the spirit. Freedom, in spite of the inflexible determinism of nature, is by no means an empty word ; it is possible, and is realised in holiness. To the saint, the world ceases to be a prison ; on the contrary, he is master of the world, because he is its highest interpreter. Through him alone the universe knows the reason for its existence, and he only realises its end.

These thoughts and many more, but in systematic combination, form what I will

call my philosophy. My friend Oliveira
Martins has made me out a Buddhist.[1]
There is, I must confess, much in common
between my doctrines and those of Buddhism ;
but still I believe the former contain something more than the latter. To my mind
this is the tendency of modern thought,
which, given its direction and starting-points,
cannot escape from Naturalism, as its every
endeavour to do so is succeeded by still
further discomfiture, except through the
door of Psychodynamism or Panpsychism.
This I believe is the nucleus, the centre
of attraction of the great nebula of modern
thought on its way to condensation. Every-
where, but particularly in Germany, I find
evident traces of this tendency. The West
will therefore in its turn bring forth its
Buddhism, its definitive mystic doctrine,

[1] *Vide* Preface to the *Sonetos Completos.*

but on more lasting foundations, and under conditions in every way more favourable, than was the case with the East.

I do not know whether, much as I wish it, I shall ever succeed in reducing my philosophical ideas to a system. I should like to concentrate on this great work the whole energy of the years that I may still have to live, but I have no confidence in my ability to carry it out. The complaint that attacks my nervous system compels me to abstain from so great, so persistent an effort as would be indispensable to bring such an important undertaking to a successful issue. I shall die, though, with the satisfaction of having foreseen the eventual direction of European thought, of having beheld from a distance the Polar Star that attracts the needle of the divine compass of the human mind. But I shall also die, after a life so full of moral agitation and sorrow, in the serene repose of thoughts closely connected with the innermost longings of the human soul, —die, as the ancients used to say, in the peace of the Lord. This is what I hope.

The last twenty-one Sonnets of my little book reflect this my final state of mind, and represent symbolically and emotionally my present views upon the world and human life. It is very little as compared with a subject so comprehensive, but to produce anything more or better was beyond my power. Poetical composition was always something quite involuntary with me, and therefore I have at least this advantage, that my verses have ever been written in perfect sincerity. I prize this little volume of Sonnets, because, like the record of a private diary, and with no more consideration than the accuracy of such daily entries demands, it accompanies the successive phases of my life, whether intellectual or emotional. It forms a kind of autobiography of thought, and, as it were, the memoirs of a conscience.

My reason for entering into such extensive biographical explanations is the consciousness that the greater part of the interest likely to be inspired by the perusal of these Sonnets would be otherwise lost. German critics may perhaps find it interesting to observe the effects of Germanism on the unprepared mind of a Southerner[1] and a descendant of the Catholic navigators of the sixteenth century. This phenomenon will possibly furnish another section, though but an unimportant one, in the history of

---

[1] In appearance Anthero belonged to a Northern type, with his fair skin, flaxen hair, and blue eyes. His family, indeed, is said to have been of French origin.

Germanism in Europe, and attract the attention of those who study the comparative psychology of nations.

I am, etc.,

ANTHERO DE QUENTAL.

THE SONNETS

1860—1862

Chorosos versos meus . . .

. . . .

Se os ditosos vos lêrem sem ternura,
Lêr—vos—hão com ternura os desgraçados.

BOCAGE, *Sonnet* II.

HAT mortal loveliness is like to thee,
    Thou vision dreamt of by mine
       ardent sprite,
That dost reflect in me thy vasty light,
E'en as the sun is mirrored in the sea?

The world is wide—my longing counsels me
Seek thee on earth: but though, poor faithful
    wight,
I search below a pitying God to sight,
His altar, old and bare, is all I see.

What I adore in thee is not of earth.
What art thou here? a kindly glance in need,
A drop of honey in a poisoned bowl:

Pure essence of the tears I weep sans dearth,
Dream of my dreams, if thou be Truth indeed,
Show thee in heaven, at least, dream of my soul!

A LAMENT

 SEA of light descends the mountain-
  side ;
  The day, the sun, that spouse
  beloved, is here !
There 's not a care in all the world so wide
That dares amid the earth-bathing light appear !

An icebound gulf or troubled ocean tide,
A struggling flower upon a hill-top drear,
Where doth the being so God-forsaken bide,
Whose prayer for peace the heavens refuse to
  hear ?

God is a father ! the All-Father too :
His love embraces every creature born :
He ne'er forgets the wrongs his children rue.

Ah ! if God give his sons good hap as wage
This sacred hour, and I cannot but mourn ;
I 'm like a son reft of his heritage !

SONNETS

TO SANTOS VALENTE

HOW small through life the cup of
pleasure is !
But deep as seas are deep and wide
as wide,
In joys unfruitful as their endless tide,
The bitter chalice of unhappiness.

And yet our souls but fruitful love and bliss
Demand of life as through the world they glide,
And pilgrims, full of doubting, they confide
In no vain hope as fully as in this.

This mighty yearning is God's high decree,
And still Illusion must impose on Life,
It gives us darkness, bids us seek the dawn !

Ah ! since the All-Father centred such a sea
Of love and grief within us 'mid the strife,
Why was the mirage made or why withdrawn ?

THE TORMENT OF THE IDEAL

 KNEW the Loveliness that never dies
And yet was sad. For as a man
may see
From lofty mount oceans and earth so wee,
And thence the tallest tower or ship espies

Grow less, and vanish 'neath the brightening skies,
E'en so the world and all appeared to me
To lose its hue, like clouds that o'er the sea
Make journey as the sun to slumber hies.

Asking of forms, in vain, the Ideal pure,
I stumble in the dark on matter dure,
And see how crude are all things that exist.

Such baptism as poets get was mine,
Amid imperfect shapes I sit and pine,
And ever have remained pallid and triste.

SONNETS

TO FLORIDO TELLES

 F power I compare or gold or fame,
    Good fortunes that conceal a wicked
      guile,
With that supreme affection for awhile
Known as true love and light of purest flame,

I see that they are like an artful dame
Who hides deceit under an honest smile,
And he that follows them an imbecile,
Leaving who loveth him for pleasure's name.

That sterile joy is born of arrogance,
And all its glory is but a deceit,
Like his that bears the palm for vanity :

From passion springs its fairest radiance,
And passion's boisterous storms soon cover it,
But love is soul-born in its majesty !

TO JOÃO DE DEUS

F 'tis a law which rules o'er thought
obscure
That searching after verity is vain,
That in light's stead we must to dark attain,
And every gain must failure fresh insure ;

'Tis law besides, though torment cruel and dure,
That we should ever seek for what is plain,
And only hold as clear and certain gain,
That which our reason long has rendered sure.

What is the soul to choose 'midst wiles so great ?
For now it doth believe and then suspect ;
It seeks, but meets with nought save vanity !

God is our only help in such a fate :
Let us eternity's clear light expect,
Be this world Exile, heaven our Destiny !

SONNETS

TO ALBERTO TELLES

LONE ! the hermit on the mountain-
side
God visiteth and gives him con-
fidence :
The sailor, tossed by storms and in suspense
At sea, a favouring breeze from heaven doth bide.

Alone ! yet he whom seas and land divide
From friends in memory hath a sure defence :
And God hath left him with at least the sense
Of hope who sobs alone at eventide.

He 's not alone who, grief and toil despite,
Hath still one tie that binds him to this life,
A faith, a wish—e'en an anxiety.

But he that folds his arms, disdainful wight,
Or stalks alone amid the crowded strife,
He 's the forsaken one, the solitary !

TO J. FELIX DOS SANTOS

LWAYS the future, and the present
ne'er !
Oh, be this hour of life with misery
And doubt ever the wretchedst, and be
Desire but sated by a good not there !

Ah ! what imports the future if, as e'er,
That hour arrives which we have longed to see,
Inclement, and but waits on grief to flee ?
And so what hope of ours is not a snare ?

Unhappiness or madness ?   What I chase,
Deceitful mirage is, if it but fly,
Worse if it wait, a spectre foul and base.

E'en thus our life must loiter and pass by ;
The present sighing for the future's face ;
The future e'er a phantom and a lie !

SONNETS

TO GERMANO MEYRELLES

ILLS only meet us, nought but grief
    exists,
    And joys are only born of fantasy ;
Of nothing but a dream our good consists,
Each moment, hour, and day is misery.

If we search for what is, what ought to be
By nature's law in smallest way assists ;
Save sadness, there is left no remedy
For him who to a mind-born good e'er lists.

Oh that we had the power to travel through
Life in a dream, nought seeing, sure 'twere best !
But 'twould be labour lost amid the unseen !

Had we the hap to lose all memory too ;
E'en then our ills would not be lulled to rest,
For to have lived the worst has ever been !

AD AMICOS

N vain we strive.   As in a misty space
The uncertainty of things our mind
involves,
Our soul as it creates, as it revolves,
Ensnares itself in its own net's embrace.

For thought, which many cunning plans will trace
A vapour is that vanishing dissolves :
And the ambitious purpose that resolves,
Breaks like a wave upon the headland's face.

Our soul is as a hymn to liberty,
To light, to fruitful good, ye Sons of Love,
The prayer and cry of foresight heavenly ;

But in a desert with deep barren bed,
Our voices echo back, and Destiny
Hovers impassible and mute o'erhead.

1862—1866

TO love ! but with a love that has some
    life,
  And not those weak arpeggios some
    admire,
Not only wild delirium and desire
Of foolish heads made hot with passion's strife.

A love that lives and glows ! a light that 's rife
To fill my being, not a kiss of fire
Snatched in the air—delirium and desire—
But love . . . of those amours that have some life.

Yes, warm and vivid ! then the light of day
Will not dispel it, claspèd to my breast,
As though it were an empty fantasy :

Nor the sun's lifted torch its strength deprive ;
For what can heavenly bodies do, at best,
Against the weakest loves . . . if they 're alive ?

A VISIT

ITH prickly thistle-flowers my room
    was starred,
    I scented me with fragrant musk
    and sweet,
And, robed in glowing purple to the feet,
I conned my canzons over like a bard :

My face and hands anointed were with nard
Brought from an Eastern garden, as was meet,
With fitting pomp and dignity to greet
The visit I had looked and longed for hard.

But what king's daughter was it, or what fay,
Or angel else, that thus came down to me,
Inside the humid dwelling where I lay?

Nor yet princess, nor fay. Nay, flower fair,
That knock was but the memory of thee
At my love's golden gate bright sans compare !

SONNETS

LITTLE ONE

 KNOW they call thee '*little one*'
full oft,

Fine as the veil in dancing dis-
arrayed,

That thou art not as yet in judgment staid,
And that thy childish frocks are scarcely doffed.

That thou 'rt a rill of water slight and soft,
The linden leaf that to and fro is swayed,
The breast with running that 's soon weary made,
The head that bends when breezes suffering waft.

But, daughter, there where I 've been wandering
Among the hills, I grew so full of fear
The Infinite's deep echoes listening to,

That I don't wish to rule or be a king,
But that thy breast should be my kingdom dear,
And all thy dolls my subjects—this I do !

71

AN EASTERN DREAM

AT times I dream I rule an isle of mine,
Far distant, planted in an Eastern
sea,
Where the clear night is full of fragrancy,
And o'er the water the full moon doth shine.

Vanilla's and magnolia's perfume fine
Floats in an air of breathless clarity,
The sea with frothy ripples, lazily,
The strand is lapping at the wood's confine.

And while against an ivory balcon's side
I lean, and muse from morn till eventide,
Thou 'rt wandering in the moonlight clear, my
sweet,

The tangled gardens through, from glade to glade,
Or resting underneath the palm-tree's shade,
With a pet lion outstretched before thy feet.

SONNETS

AN IDYLL

HEN we set out, we twain, our hands
    clasped tight,
    Lilies and daisies plucking in the
    vale,
When at a bound the hill's long side we scale
Still wet and sparkling with the dews of night;

Or, seaward looking from some lonesome height,
Gaze at the evening clouds, as day doth fail,
That, pilèd up on the horizon pale,
Seem like fantastic ruins to the sight:

How often, suddenly, thy speech doth go,
And in thine eyes a strange light fluctuates!
I feel thy hand shake, see thee pallid grow:

I hear the murmured prayer of seas and winds,
And poetry from all things saturates,
So lovingly and slow, our hearts and minds.

THE SPIRIT OF NIGHT

SPIRIT that passest, when the wind
sleeps low
　　O'er ocean and the moon is waxing
great,
Thou only know'st how cruel is my fate,
Coy son of darkness floating to and fro.

And as a song that—sorrowful and slow—
Wafted from far, doth subtly penetrate,
So o'er my heart, in tumult-troubled state,
Thou pourest out oblivion of woe.

To thee I trust the dream in which I'm borne
By instinct's light, that darkness' veil hath torn
And seeks the lasting Good where phantoms wone.

Thou knowest all my nameless misery,
The fever of the Ideal wasting me,
Thou Genius of the Night, and thou alone !

SONNETS

A DREAM

 DREAMT—and dreams are not all
empty guile—
A wind had snatched me up, and
that apace
'Twas bearing me across the starry space
Where an eternal dawn doth beauteous smile.

The stars, that wait the morn in guardian style,
E'en as with secret sorrow in my face
I passed, looked towards me with an anxious gaze,
And said : 'Where dwells our sister, friend, the
while ?'

But I cast down my eyes for fear, perforce,
They should betray the sorrow that I feel,
And furtively and silent held my course ;

Nor had I or the will or power, in fine,
To tell those stars, thy sisters pure and leal,
How false thou art, my sweet, and how indign !

75

ANTHERO DE QUENTAL

SELF-DENIAL

AY rose and lily rain thy neck
around!
And may thy soul be flooded with
a psalm
Of praise and adoration's kindly balm,
My darling dove, my hope that knows no bound!

May heaven give thee stars, and flowers the
ground,
Perfume and songs the air and shade the palm,
And when the moon is out and ocean calm,
Its lazy loitering roll a dream profound!

Oh! may'st thou ne'er remember that I mourn,
And e'en forget I love thee, poor forlorn,
And, passing me, look not from off the soil;

While, from the tears fast flowing out mine eyes,
May faithful flowers beneath thy feet uprise,
For thee to careless crush, or smiling spoil.

SONNETS

A SPECTRE

ONE day, my love—for now I see it loom,
  E'en now I feel my heart is breaking fast !—
Thou wilt remember, pitiful at last,
The tender oaths I made, fearing my doom.

Then in the secret corner of a room,
Beneath the lamp that flickering rays doth cast,
I 'll rise up like a phantom of the past,
A ghost escaped its exile in the tomb.

And thou, at seeing me, with many a sigh
And groan, with outstretched arms and eager face
Wilt seek to grasp my garments then and cry,

'Oh ! listen ! wait ! '—but I 'll refuse to hear,
And, dreamlike, fleeing from thy dear embrace,
As smoke amid the air will disappear !

A MOTHER

A MOTHER—to compose my life of
    pain,
  To watch this chilly night about my
    bed,
And with her pitying hands retie the thread
Of my poor being, nearly cut in twain.

To bear me at her bosom, overta'en
By sleep, when passing places dark and dread,
And in the stream of clear effulgence shed
By her dear glance to cleanse my soul from stain.

For this I 'd give my manly pride, and eke
My fruitless knowledge, careless of the rest,
I 'd turn me to a little child and weak,

And be as happy, docile, without fear,
If I could take my sleep upon thy breast,
If only thou couldst be my mother, dear !

SONNETS

THE PALACE OF HAPPINESS

IN dreams an Errant Knight I seem
to be.
   Through deserts, under suns, by
night obscure,
Love's paladin, I search for eagerly
The enchanted house of Happiness secure !

But now I 'm faint and worn and like to flee,
My sword is broken, armour insecure,
When lo I sight it shining, suddenly,
In all its pomp and airy formosure !

With many a blow I strike the gate and cry :
'The Wanderer, the Disherited am I !
Ye gates of gold, to my complaining ope!'

With a loud noise the golden gates fly wide,
But nothing meets my sorrowing gaze inside,
Save deathlike calm, and darkness without hope.

AN OATH

Y wrinkles on a forehead deep in
thought,
And by the questioning look that
nought can see,
And by the icy hand of misery
That has eclipsed the star our soul's eye sought ;

And by the crackling of a flame distraught,
Amid the failing fire's last agony,
By the fierce cry of one who 's left to dree
The ruin swift her lover on her brought ;

By all things fateful, all that mingled shade
And terror, that beneath a gravestone lies ;
O gentle dove of esperance ever-green !

I swear to thee I 've seen, and been afraid
Of horrors—but a thing in any wise
More cruel than a child's laugh I 've never seen !

SONNETS

WHILST OTHERS FIGHT

WERE I to grasp the sword the valiant
    bear,
    And rush into the fight, intoxicate,
In that dread battle-field, where Death and Fate
Give laws to trembling Kings, and nations dare !

And were my lungs to breathe the fiery air
The arena, stained with blood, gives forth, elate ;
Were I to fall, shrouded in radiance great
By glittering sword-blades with their tawny glare !

I should not have to see the morning pale
Of my so useless years and hourly wail
Them spent in nought save dreams and bitterness !

Nor watch while, in my very hand undone,
The roses fall to pieces, one by one,
Of this my sterile youth and colourless !

DESPONDENCY

H let it go, the bird from which they 've ta'en
Both nest and young, its all, sans ruth or care,
And be it carried by the boundless air,
On parted wings, from solitary pain !

Oh let it go, the ship the hurricane
Has whirled across the ocean, loath to spare,
When darkest night came down from out its lair,
And when the winds rose from the Southern main !

Oh let it go, the soul that, full of gloom,
Has lost all trust and all its peace, for aye,
To silent death and to the restful tomb !

Oh let it go, the ending note and slow
Of a last song, and then hope's final ray . . .
And life . . and love, as well . . Oh let life go !

SONNETS

DAS UNNENBARE

CHIMERA, thou that passest cradled
  right
  Amid the wavelet of my dreams of
  woe,
And brushest with thy vapoury vesture's flow
My forehead pale and weary of the light !

Thou 'rt carried by the air of peaceful night :
In vain, with anxious mien, I seek to know
What name on thee the venturesome bestow
In thine own country, mystic fairy wight !

But what a fate is mine ! What a dim glow
This dawn brings, like that at the sun's last pace,
When only livid clouds float to and fro !

For night grants no illusion, and I seem
To view thee far off only when I dream,
And even then I cannot see thy face !

A WOMAN FRIEND

Y dear ones have been scattered by
some wind,
  I see them not, I know not where
they wone,
I stretch my arms out when the light has flown,
And kiss the phantoms called up by my mind.

While others cause me pangs of sharper kind
Than yearning for the dead, whose lot alone
I envy, for they pass as if they 'd grown
Ashamed of me, unfriended, and declined !

Of all that happy spring-time once enjoyed
No flower is left, not e'en a rose, to-day ;
The wind has swept them off, the frost destroyed !

But thou wast faithful, and, as in the past,
Thou turnest still thine eyes, so bright and gay,
To see my tale of ills—and mock at last !

SONNETS

THE VOICE OF AUTUMN

'IST thou, my wearied heart, attentively,
 To Nature's voice and words to thee,
  forlorn :
' It had been better if thou hadst been born
'Mid deserts drear, in helpless nudity,

If thou hadst made thy moan in infancy
Upon a cheerless pasture place and lorn,
If Beauty's Fairy had not, night and morn,
Within Illusion's cradle dandled thee !

Better if silent, and with grief down-bowed,
Thy visionary soul its way had ta'en
Amid the hostile world, the varying crowd,

(Of all thou hast loved not seeing one sole flower)
By hate and sorrow torn—than, to thy bane,
To have dreamt ideal dreams hour after hour ! '

ANTHERO DE QUENTAL

A ROMANTIC BURYING-PLACE

WHERE the great sea breaks, with a
  swirl and roar
  Monotonous, 'tis there my heart
  shall find
Its place of sepulture, and where the wind
Uplifts its lamentation on the shore.

And let the summer suns their rays outpour
Upon it, day by day, in lingering kind,
In winter-time let blasts, with fury blind,
Toss up around it the dry sandy floor,

Until it is undone, and then, resolved
In finest dust, oh, let it be revolved
Amid the whirlwinds lifted by the breeze,

And swallowed up at last with all its pain,
Its weariness and strife, its loves insane,
In those unfruitful tides and bitter seas !

1864—1874

V

BUT what is the Ideal? Who has
    seen
      Once, only once, this hidden pilgrim
    wight?
And who has kissed her hand of heavenly might,
Or clothed him with her loving glance's sheen?

Pale image that some rivulet serene,
Reflecting, carries off with it, a light
So dubious that it barely comes in sight,
A cloud the air brought and bore off at e'en.

Oh haste to meet her then, your arms upraise
Lean from the fever deepest musing's birth,
All ye who follow her through boundless space !

And yet my weeping Soul and sorrow-sure,
Thou hast no other love through all the earth
Than this disdainful virgin, icy pure !

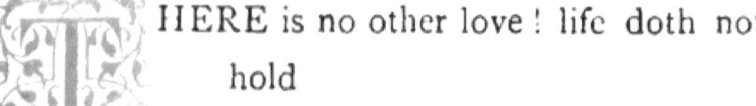HERE is no other love ! life doth not
    hold
    A better shelter for our heads in lieu,
Nor yet a sweeter balsam and more true
To heal our wound of centuries untold !

For whether she fly coyly, or make bold
To yield, as one that loves and tells it too,
And whether she be clouded or in view,
She will be e'er the promised spouse of old !

To thee, O cold one, rise our longings aye,
E'en as the arms of a poor exiled wight
Towards his fatherland, by night and day.

If thou dost flee, our soul, delirious,
Will follow thee across the infinite,
Till it returns with thee, victorious :

VII

H what a wondrous marriage that will
    be !
  How glorious ! when the Heavens
    form the bed
Of love, and where are pendent overhead
The stars for curtains and a canopy !

The bridal of Desire all frenzied by
Good luck at last, and visions fiery red
Of one that goes to fervent fancies wed,
Caught up and carried through immensity !

There, where imagination ends its sway
'Mid dreams of beauty far beyond our ken,
And where the night is brighter than our day ;

There, in the bosom of eternal light,
Where God gives answer to the voice of men,
We shall embrace thee, Truth, and win our right !

VIII

BUT where is *there?* The sky of the
    Idea,
    The sky the faithful soul doth con-
    stant pray
And long for, my unconquered heart, I say
Thou vainly seekest in this boundless sphere !

For Space is mute ; the immensity austere
In vain is lighted up by night and day.
The roses of a spring to last for aye
In not a star or sun do yet appear !

And Paradise with Truth's immortal fane,
Oh worlds unnumbered, suns and starry zone,
None of you have it in your endless reign !

But the Ideal, the Word, the Essence and
The Greatest Good reveal themselves alone
To man beneath the sky of Conscience-land !

SONNETS

WORDS OF ONE OF THE DEAD

'VE lain here dead upon the mountain
    crest
    A thousand years, exposed to wind
    and rain ;
As lean as I there is no spectre vain,
Nor an abortion more deformed.   At best

My spirit only lives, on guard, oppressed
By one fixed thought of never-ending bane ;
'Buried alive !' my constant torturing pain
Is only this—no matter for the rest.

I know I lived once . . . though but for a day,
No more . . . and then Idolatry, for aye,
Gave altars and a cult . . . they worshipped me

As though I had been *Some one* ! just as though
Life could be *Some one* !—afterwards, oh woe !
They said I was a God . . . and shrouded me !

TO A POET

CALM spirit, that beneath the cedar-tree
    Bent down with years, art resting,
    slumber-swayed,
E'en as a Levite in the altar's shade,
Far from the noisy strife of earth and free.

Awake ! 'tis time !   The sun in majesty
Has put to flight the ghosts, the spectres laid,
And a new world waits but the signal made
To rise from out the bosom of the sea.

List thou ! for 'tis the people's clamouring !
And they who rise, thy brethren !   Lo they sing
A battle-song, and give the alarm afar !

Up, soldier of the Future, rise at last,
And from the rays that purest dreams have cast,
Thou dreamer, forge thyself a sword for war !

1874—1880

SONNETS

MORS LIBERATRIX

WITHIN thine hand, O sombre cavalier,
    All girt about with armour black as
        night,
    There gleams a falchion forged of
        comets bright,
That rends the veil of dark with rays most clear.

Pursuing thine adventurous career,
Clothed in a thick and self-projected night,
The tawny ribbon of thy sword of light
Alone emerges from the fog so drear.

'This sword I wield is shimmering and stark
(Makes answer that Knight Errant of the Dark)
Because it is the sword of Verity.

I slay, but save ; I conquer and lay low,
And yet console ; I ransom if o'erthrow ;
And, being Death, am also Liberty.'

ANTHERO DE QUENTAL

MORS—AMOR

HAT coal-black steed, whose tramp
  of fearful might
  I hear in dreams, when darkness
  cloaks the sky,
Whom at full gallop I have seen pass by
On the fantastic causeways of the night,—

Whence comes he? or what regions out of sight
And full of terrors has he crossed, or why
Seems he so dark and wondrous to the eye,
Why tosses he his mane as though affright?

A cavalier of dread and mighty gest,
Whose port is calm yet terrible to view,
From head to foot in shining armour dressed,

Bestrides that mystic beast all fearlessly,
And the black courser neighs, ' I'm Death!' and
    you?
· 'Tis I am Love!' his rider makes reply!

SONNETS

MY SOUL

RIM Death was there a little way
ahead,

Confronting me, so like unto a
snake

That sleeping on the highway doth awake,

And dart up as she feels the traveller's tread.

That fell bacchante, with her gesture dread

And devilish, was a sight at which to quake !

And when I asked, 'Thou ravening beast, whose
wake

Art following through the world?' she only said.

'Fear not' (and then a sort of irony,

Most sinister and yet most calm, did roll

And writhe a mouth that spoke of cruelty)

''Tis not thy body I am seeking—No !

That were too great a trophy——'Tis thy soul.'

'My soul,' I made reply, 'died long ago.'

THE DIVINE COMEDY

EN lift their arms to heaven from out
the fray,
Apostrophise the powers invisible,
And make their moan—'Ye Gods impassible,
Whom e'en triumphant fate must needs obey,

Why did ye make us? Since, from day to day,
Time flies, and but begets unquenchable
Illusion, Grief and Sin, Strifes horrible,
All in a whirl of frenzy and dismay.

Were it not better in the kindly peace
Of Nothingness, and of what is not yet,
To have stayed and slept a sleep that cannot
cease?

Why have ye called us forth to sorrow thus?'
To which, in tones of even more regret,
The Gods reply, 'O Men! why made ye us?'

SONNETS

NOX

 NIGHT, my thoughts fly to thee and
    thy reign,
  When, by the cruel glare of day, I
    see
So much vain striving, so much agony,
So many bitter torments all in vain.

Thou stiflest at the least those cries of pain
The dungeon yields, brimful of tragedy ;
The ever-raging roaring Ill in thee
Reposes, and forgets awhile its bane.

But oh ! that thou wouldst fall asleep as well,
Once and for aye, and, changeless then as fate,
Forget thee with the World beneath thy spell,

And that the World, all seeing striving o'er,
Would sleep upon thy breast inviolate,
Night of Non-being, Night for evermore !

ON THE JOURNEY

UPON the narrow path, near which 'tis
    rare
    To see a flower or bird, or sip one
    taste
Of water, where are rugged rocks and bare,
Or deserts parched, a fever-stricken waste,

I entered straightway with a fearless air,
And, seeing them in front, all fearless faced
The ghosts that on the horizon, from their lair,
Rose up to combat my stout heart in haste.

Who are ye, mystic pilgrims here below?
Grief, Disillusion, Weariness and Woe;
And Death is watching still behind the crew.

I know you, the last guides that I shall need,
My silent comrades and my friends indeed :
Oh, welcome all, and thou, Death, welcome too !

SONNETS

QUIA AETERNUS

THOU hast not died, though vain
 philosophy
 Full proudly vaunts the fact to all
 mankind,
The yoke and reins of heavenly tyranny
Are not so straight and easy to unbind!

An empty boast, for this great victory
That Reason revels in—effete and blind—
Of thine eternal tragic irony
Is but a novel form, one more unkind.

Spectre, thou art not dead! Thought, as of yore,
Must face thee; thou 'rt the bane of all that pore
And puzzle over books from year to year.

And those who love debauchery, alas!
How oft it haps that, as they raise the glass,
They pause, and, trembling, pallid grow for fear!

IN THE WHIRLWIND

WHILST I am dreaming ghostly forms
file by,
The creatures of my thoughts, e'en
as a band
Swept onward by the winds from land to land,
And in their vasty whirl caught up on high.

Wreathed in a wondrous spiral, whence a cry
And weird lamenting echoes o'er the strand,
They pass, a shadowy group, and, as I stand,
I catch their features now and then, and sigh.

O phantoms of my self and soul, whose mien
Is dreadful calm, a terror to have seen,
Borne forward on the troubled billow's breast,

My brethren and my butchers, who are ye?
Avenging ghosts, the spirit of misery?
Ah me! ah me! and who am I at best?

SONNETS

IGNOTUS

WHERE art thou hiding ? Lo, our
fruitless prayer
As we sigh on, and raise our hands
in vain !
Now hoarse our voices grow, our hearts with strain
Are weary—and we give up in despair.

We seek o'er seas and lands, through heaven so fair,
The Spirit that fills space ; and, full of pain,
Our voices only echo back again
Amid the solitude . . . thou art not there !

Whither ? and where ? ye heavens and earth make
cry—
But the ancient Spirit only gives reply,
In tones of weariness and woe combined :

'Cease your complaint, sons of perplexity,
For I myself, from all eternity,
Do also seek myself—but cannot find !'

IN THE CIRCUS

FAR hence, and yet I know not when
or where
That world was that I lived in, nor
the way,
But 'twas so distant I could almost say
That I was dreaming whilst I movèd there.

For all things were aerial and fair,
And being dawned upon me bright and gay,
And I was as the light, until, one day,
A wind caught up and whirled me in mid-air.

I fell and found me suddenly engaged,
There where at large a brutal fury raged,
In bestial strife upon the circus floor :

I felt a monster grow inside of me,
And saw I'd turned wild beast quite suddenly ;
And hence it is I with the lions roar !

SONNETS

NIRVÂNA

BEYOND this Universe so luminous,
    So full of forces and of forms,
      oppressed
By noisy strife and longings vain at best,
A realm lies open dark and vacuous.

The billows of this sea tumultuous,
Retired into themselves, come there and rest ;
In boundless immobility and blest
There Being ends for each and all of us.

And when Thought, thus absorbed and occupied,
Hard though it be, from this dead world hath hied,
And turns to look at Nature once again,

At lifetime's loveliest light so limitless,
It only sees, o'ercome by weariness,
That all things are illusory and vain !

1880—1884

 OW that the strife is o'er, in peaceful
state
My heart is resting free from fear
of bane,
I 've come at length to understand 'tis vain
The good disputed with the World and Fate.

With fevered brow oft did I penetrate
Into the sanctum of Illusion's fane,
And only found, confused and pierced by pain,
Darkness and dust, brute matter desolate.

There is not in the world's immensity—
Though great it seems in early manhood viewed—
Aught that our souls' desire can satisfy.

There 'mid the unseen and the intangible,
O'er deserts, vacuum and solitude,
The Spirit floats above impassible!

EVOLUTION

 WAS a rock, and, on a distant day,
 A trunk or tree-branch in a wood
 unknown ;
A wave, I broke against the granite stone,
My oldest enemy, in clouds of spray.

I roared, a beast perhaps, upon the way
To shelter in some cave all heather-grown ;
Or, ancient monster, raised my head alone
'Mid reedy marshes, where my pasture lay.

Now I 'm a man—and, in the densest shade,
I see, below, the stair of many a grade
That, spiralwise, goes down the immensity ;

The Infinite I call on and weep sore ;
But, stretching out my hands in space, adore
And yearn for nothing else than liberty.

SONNETS

IN PRAISE OF DEATH

I

FT the Inconscient, at night's midmost pace,
    Shakes me with force, and I awake in fright,
My heart, as if crushed by a blow, poor wight,
Although no weakling, pauses in its race.

Not that my mind fills full of ghouls this space,
This vacuum of still and awful night,
That reason forces it to put to flight
Some pangs remorseful it dare hardly face.

No visionary ghosts of night I spy,
No mortuary phantoms filing by,
Nor yet of God and Fate a fear I feel.

Nothing! the bottom of a warm dank well,
Curtained around by gloom, a silent spell,
And Death's sepulchral footsteps at my heel.

II

Y painful thoughts immure themselves
  and me,
  Each day, in dreamland's forest
  undefined.
Through realms of vague oblivion and blind,
Step after step, I'm led by fantasy.

I pierce at dark the chilly mist, and see
A world of wonders peopled by the wind,
While full of doubt and querulous my mind
Trusts but the ghosts of night full hopefully.

What mystical desire distracts me so?
Nirvâna's deep abyss appears below,
Confronting me, so silent and so vast!

And as I traverse solitary space,
I only seek to meet thee and embrace,
Sister of Love and Truth, thou, Death, at last!

SONNETS

III

KNOW not who thou art, yet do not
  seek,
  So great my trust is, to discover it,
Enough among night's forms with whom I
  speak,
If thou beside me in the dark dost sit.

Across the stillness full of gloom and bleak
Thy steps I follow, fearing not a whit,
Right o'er the chasm of the Future, eke,
I lean me at thy voice, to fathom it.

For thee engulfed amid the world of night
Where phantoms dwell, and on a nameless strand,
I try to fix thy wondrous gaze aright.

To fix and fathom it an hour's enow,
Funereal Beatrice with the icy hand,
The one consoling Beatrice here below!

IV

 GUESSED not long (what mist in-
  vincible
  Blinded my spirit, this I may not
  know !)
Who 'twas that by my side did constant go,
By day and night, comrade impassible.

Ofttime, 'tis true, amid the unbearable
Extremest tedium of a life of woe,
To thee I gave a troubled look, and so
Invoked thee, my last friend most peaceable.

But then I loved thee not nor knew indeed;
My weak and listless mind could nothing read
On this calm countenance, this silent scroll.

But now, enlightened by an inner flame,
Child of the selfsame sire, I know thy name,
Death, co-eternal sister of my soul !

SONNETS

 PECTRE austere, how shall I name
    thee, pray,
  Whom at the high-road's turning,
    undismayed,
I spy, e'en as my soul's poor strength doth fade,
And she is worn and weary of the way?

The crowd sees in thine eyes a gulf, and aye
It hides its visage, and draws back afraid,
But I confide in thee, thou veilèd shade,
And think I understand what thou dost say.

And, step by step, I see appear more bright
In thy profoundest gaze that ne'er doth cease,
The sign of the Ideal, daughter of night.

I 'll sleep upon thy breast changeless as fate,
In the communion of a world-wide peace,
O liberating Death inviolate!

VI

E only whom Non-being doth affright
    Feareth thy silence vast and mor-
      tuary,
Night without end and space most solitary,
Thou night of Death, the dark and dreadsome
    hight,

Not I ; my humble soul yet full of might
Thy hall of mourning enters faithfully ;
To others thou art ashes, vacancy,
For me thy gloomy face hath smiles most bright.

I love the holy peace ineffable,
The peerless silence of the Unchangeable,
That cloaks the eternal good in mourning suit :

Non-being though 'twere wrong to seek thee out,
One yet may worship thee and dream about,
The only Being true and absolute.

SONNETS

LACRYMAE RERUM

 NIGHT, Death's sister, Reason's
constant mate,
How many times I've questioned
anxiously,
Thine oracle of deepest sanctity,
Thou gossip and interpreter of Fate !

Where go thy suns, like to a cohort great
Of restless souls led on by Destiny?
And why, so vainly seeking certainty
To comfort him, doth man walk desolate?

But, 'mid the pomp of this great funeral,
The ill-boding night-time, still and masterful,
Goes on its course and turns the lazy hours.

I'm compassed round by doubt, and grief is near ;
And, lost amid an endless dream, I hear
The sigh that comes from where the darkness
lowers.

ANTHERO DE QUENTAL

REDEMPTION

I

OICES of wood and wind, and ocean's
    cry,
  When sometimes, in my dreaming
    dolorous,
I'm cradled by your song so mighteous,
I think ye suffer e'en as much as I.

O inmost life, expression peeping sly
From silent things; O psalm mysterious;
O art thou not, complaint so nebulous,
The world's lament from out the strife and sigh?

A spirit dwells within the immensity;
A cruel and poignant lust for liberty
Shivers and shakes all transient forms that be :

And well I understand your language strange,
Voices of ocean, wood, and mountain range,
Ye sister souls to mine, captive like me !

SONNETS

II

E oceans, winds, and woods, mourn
    not your doom,
    Ye ancient choir of voices mur-
    muring,
Of voices primitive and saddening
E'en as the wail of spectres from the tomb.

Where glimmering ghosts bemoan from out the
    gloom
You will break forth one day all glittering,
From out this dream and shameful suffering,
Which your complaints so mystical unwomb.

Souls in the limbo of existence yet,
To Knowledge you 'll awake and freedom get,
And hovering high above, pure Pensament,

Behold the Forms, Illusion's children vain,
Undone and fall to earth like dreams inane,
And then at length your tortures will be spent.

STRIFE

NIGHT slumbers resting on the hilly
    steep.
    Like to a dream, oblivious save of
    peace,
The moon mounts higher. The winds sink and
    cease,
And plain and vale have ta'en a common sleep.

But as for me, the night, whilome a keep
Of sympathies divine, my thought doth freeze
With fear, and shadowy troops around increase,
The Fates and pilgrim Spirits crowding deep!

Unfathomable problem! Full of fright
My mind recoils! And now, when prostrate quite
And stupefied with weariness and ill,

Inconscient I watch the ghostly band,
Whilst up and down the solitary strand
Thine ancient voice, O sea, doth echo still.

SONNETS

LOGOS

HOU whom I see not, yet who art
quite close,
    Nay more, within me, folding me
inside
A cloud of feelings and ideas so wide,
Which my beginning, middle, end, compose,

How strange a being (if being, as I suppose),
That thus doth snatch me up, and by thy side
Mak'st me to walk where fear and joy divide
The rule, in realms of yeses and of noes.

But a reflection of my soul thou art,
And, 'stead of facing thee unmoved, I start,
And trembling supplicate on seeing thee.

I speak, thou 'rt mute ; I stop, thou listenest ;
Thou 'rt sire and brother, yet thou torturest
When nigh—a tyrant, and I worship thee !

WITH THE DEAD

THOSE I have loved, where are they? gone from sight,
    Dragged headlong by the tempest's whirling blind,
And borne, as in a dream, 'mong phantom-kind,
Amid the world's so swiftly rushing flight.

Whilst I myself, with feet immersed, poor wight,
And at the mercy of the stream and wind,
But livid surging foam around me find,
And here and there drowned faces meet my sight.

Yet if I pause awhile, and only can
Seal up mine eyes, I feel them at my side
Again, my dear ones, living, man for man.

I see and list them, and they hear my say,
Joined in the ancient love and sanctified,
In the communion of Good for aye.

OCEANO NOX

EAR to the sea, that raised with gravity
  Its tragic voice and harsh, while rushing by
The wind went, like a thought that soars on high,
And seeks, yet hesitates, all fitfully,

Near to the sea I sat down tristfully,
And gazed a while at the dull heavy sky,
And, musing, questioned this lament and sigh
That rose from out of things uncertainly.

What restless longing tortures you, what fate,
Ye rudimental Beings, force unknown,
Round what Idea do ye gravitate?

But in far-reaching distant space, where hides
The Unconscious and Immortal One, a moan
And bitter cry makes answer, nought besides.

COMMUNION

ETHINK thee now, my soul, for I 'll repress
  My tears, what crowds have jour-
    neyed us before,
And, full of doubt, their hands raised to implore
Beneath this sky austere in their distress !

—-A light of death ! a spring that's bitterness !—
Yet still their patient hearts the strife upbore,
Believers but from instinct, they set store
By that heroic faith that e'er doth bless.

And am I more than they ? A fate like theirs
Binds me to that of multitudes unknown ;
My path I then will follow free from cares,

Amid those faces mute but of the fold,
Filled by the humble faith that ages own,
And in communion with our sires of old.

SONNETS

SOLEMNIA VERBA

 TO my heart: 'Regard the manifold
And useless paths we took! Look
back and see
Now from this height, austere and cold may be,
The desert watered by our tears untold.

Ashes and dust where flowers bloomed of old!
Where shone the spring is now obscurity!
Regard the world beneath, despairingly,
Thou author of delusions, and their hold!'

To which my heart, made valorous and strong
Within the school of constant torturing pain,
And full of faith since tried by grief and wrong,

Made answer: 'I see Love from here in wait!
If this be life, my life was not in vain,
Nor grief and disillusion were too great.

DEATH'S MESSAGE

'H ! let the toilers come to me secure ;
Oh ! suffer all the suffering to come
near ;
And those who, worn by sorrows long and sure,
Eye their vain deeds at which they mock and jeer.

In me the Sufferings harsh that have no cure,
Doubt, Passions, Evil, pass and disappear.
Grief's torturing pains that pause not, cruel and
dure,
As in an ocean, cease their heads to rear.'

Such is Death's message. Death, the veilèd Word,
The interpreter so sacred, though unheard,
Of things invisible, and cold as clay,

Is, in its silence, far more resonant,
Far, than the clamorous sea ; more rutilant,
More, in its night, than the fair light of day.

SONNETS

IN THE HAND OF GOD

 ITHIN God's hand, in His right hand,
    for aye,
    My wearied heart has found a rest
    from care.
I 've gone down step by step the narrow stair
Of the charmed Palace 'neath Illusion's sway.

And like the flowers, fading in a day,
That childish ignorance will vainly wear,
The transient forms imperfect (yet so fair !)
Of Passion and the Ideal I 've put away.

E'en as a child that dismal journey goes,
Borne at its mother's breast secure from foes,
And passes, ever smiling, through and o'er,

Forests, and desert sands, and oceans deep,—
My liberated heart, now take thy sleep
Within the hand of God for evermore !

INDEX TO THE SONNETS

ANTHERO DE QUENTAL

INDEX TO THE SONNETS

ERRATA

p. 21, l. 6—*for* Falção *read* Falcão
p. 60, ll. 2 and 3—*read*

    .   .   .   . As from a mountain he
That looks sees earth and ocean's empery,

p. 61, ll. 7 and 8—*read*

And their pursuer foolish, volatile,
As he who leaves his fair in pleasure's name.

p. 64, l. 3—*for* wretchedst *read* wretchedest
p. 66, l. 13—*for* Destiny *read* Fate above
p. 69, l. 1—*for* has some *read* speaks of
p. 69, l. 11—*read* As though it came of idle fancy's play :
p. 79, l. 6—*for* armour insecure *read* and my mail unsure,
p. 80, l. 7—*for* who's left *read* condemned
p. 80, l. 12—*read* I swear that I have seen and felt afraid
p. 80, l. 14—*read*

More fierce than childish laughter ne'er have seen.

p. 91, ll. 5 and 6—*read*

The bridal of Desire in ecstasy
With joy at last, etc.

p. 97, l. 2—*read* Girt round by coal-black armour for the fight,
p. 101, l. 1—*for* to thee *read* toward thee
p. 104, l. 13—*for* spirit *read* sport
p. 119, l. 2—*read* How often have I questioned eagerly,
p. 120, l. 3—*for* so mighteous *read* altisonous,
p. 124, l. 8—*for* meet my sight *read* come to light
p. 124, l. 14—*read* In union with the eternal Good for aye.
p. 129, ll. 7 and 8—*read*

The transient forms of Passioning and fair,
With old Ideals, I have put away.

Edinburgh : T. and A. Constable
Printers to Her Majesty